DES DILLON is an award-winning  up in Coatbridge he studied                                      at Strathclyde University and Popular Culture with Open University. Taught English in Scottish secondary schools. Was writer in residence at Castlemilk 1998-2000. He is a poet, short story writer, novelist and dramatist writing for radio, stage, television and film. He lives in Galloway.

Also by Des Dillon

*Me and Ma Gal*
*The Big Empty*
*Duck*
*Itchycooblue*
*Return Of The Busby Babes*
*The Big Q*
*Six Black Candles*

Praise for Des Dillon's poetry

**Lesley Benzie**
The authenticity, brutality, humour and most of all the humanity of the characters and the reality of the world they inhabit in Des Dillon's stories, are never in question. Neither is the talent that allows us to share a window on that world. This is mirrored in Des's debut poetry collection *Picking Brambles*. As if that alone were not enough, he gives us much more, by revealing through his poetic soul a big, big heart and a soft underbelly.

**Alan Bissett**
It has been known for years that Des Dillon writes some of Scotland's most vibrant prose, but now we can see his poetry is on the side of the angels too. This is a collection which beats with a full, tough heart, and thrums like good music. Fathers, lovers, old friends, the dispossessed, Italian nuns, schoolchildren, cello players, neds and hopeless romantics all wink out at us from the train of Dillon's thoughts. We miss every one of them like hell when they're gone.

**Jim Craig**
Des Dillon says in his introduction that he considers himself first and foremost a poet – he's right! A superb collection which easily matches his award-winning novels for quality.

**Bashabi Fraser**
'Keep looking' and in Des Dillon's poetry you will witness the patriot Scot of 'Coatbridge' and 'Cairnhill', who has not sunk into the oblivion of 'Carlsberg Specials', but is able to address grave issues like child abuse wrapped in neighbourliness or reach

out beyond the horizon to feel the pain of the hungry thousands in Leningrad. The Scottish landscape is the most beautiful in chance encounters with hovering hawks and timid deer. The poems combine the personal and political with a clever use of language (I specially like 'Photograbbed/photograbberry') to create startling metaphors in what is confessional poetry in a very modern context.

**Anne MacLeod**
Des Dillon's *Picking Brambles* is a collection that sweeps from Coatbridge via New York and Ireland to Monte Casino describing with great elegance and economy the warmth, the humanity that transcend poverty, whatever the nationality.

Known primarily as an urban voice for his work in film and fiction, Dillon is a poet whose appreciation and love of nature are evident. His spare, lyrical language resonates in the mind and heart long after the book is shut, the poems laid aside. He writes with great delicacy of love, of politics, of the joy and pain inherent in life, in living.

This collection will surprise and delight. Its freshness, its lyricism, its sheer charm and openness will ensure that Des Dillon is seen as one of Scotland's most promising poets whose particular achievement in this volume is to combine accessibility and finely honed poetic technique; heart and craft.

These poems will draw many folk back to poetry. I loved them.

**Janet Paisley**
Des Dillon's exuberant mastery of language energises everything he writes. These poems are fleshed with vibrant, fresh, exciting images that demonstrate the eye of an artist for illuminating detail, the precision of a craftsman in their exactness, and the skill of a conjurer in revealing a new-made world painted in words. The journey from cover to cover is as stunning and rewarding as

a wander round Paris' Musée d'Orsay, from realist to impressionist, with an occasional Dali-esque vision thrown in. Dillon has made a poetry that resonates with joy even in its sorrows, and revives tenderness and compassion in its view of humanity. Both sensual and spiritual, this is a seductive collection.

**Eileen Ramsay**
Dear Des, The depth and range of your poetry astonishes me. You have a genius for making the reader feel the poem is her/his experience – I read some to Ian too – I love to see the world through your eyes and I weep for our sadness in some of them and I laugh at your wit in others. There are so many that I wish I'd written, too many that made me say, 'I wish I could write like that'. Hard to choose favourites but I loved 'Picking Brambles', and 'Being', and 'Unrequited Love' and 'Garlieston' and 'Glasgow Chamber Orchestra' and and and… Thank you for asking me to read them. I look forward to the day that our grandchildren will be reading them in school. Love Eileen

# Picking Brambles
and other poems

DES DILLON

selected and introduced by
Brian Whittingham

**Luath** Press Limited
EDINBURGH
www.luath.co.uk

First published 2003

The paper used in this book is recyclable. It is made from low-chlorine pulps produced in a low-energy, low-emission manner from renewable forests.

The publisher acknowledges subsidy from

Scottish **Arts** Council

towards the publication of this volume.

Printed and bound by
Creative Print and Design, Ebbw Vale

Typeset in 10.5 point Sabon by
S. Fairgrieve, Edinburgh 0131 658 1763

© Des Dillon

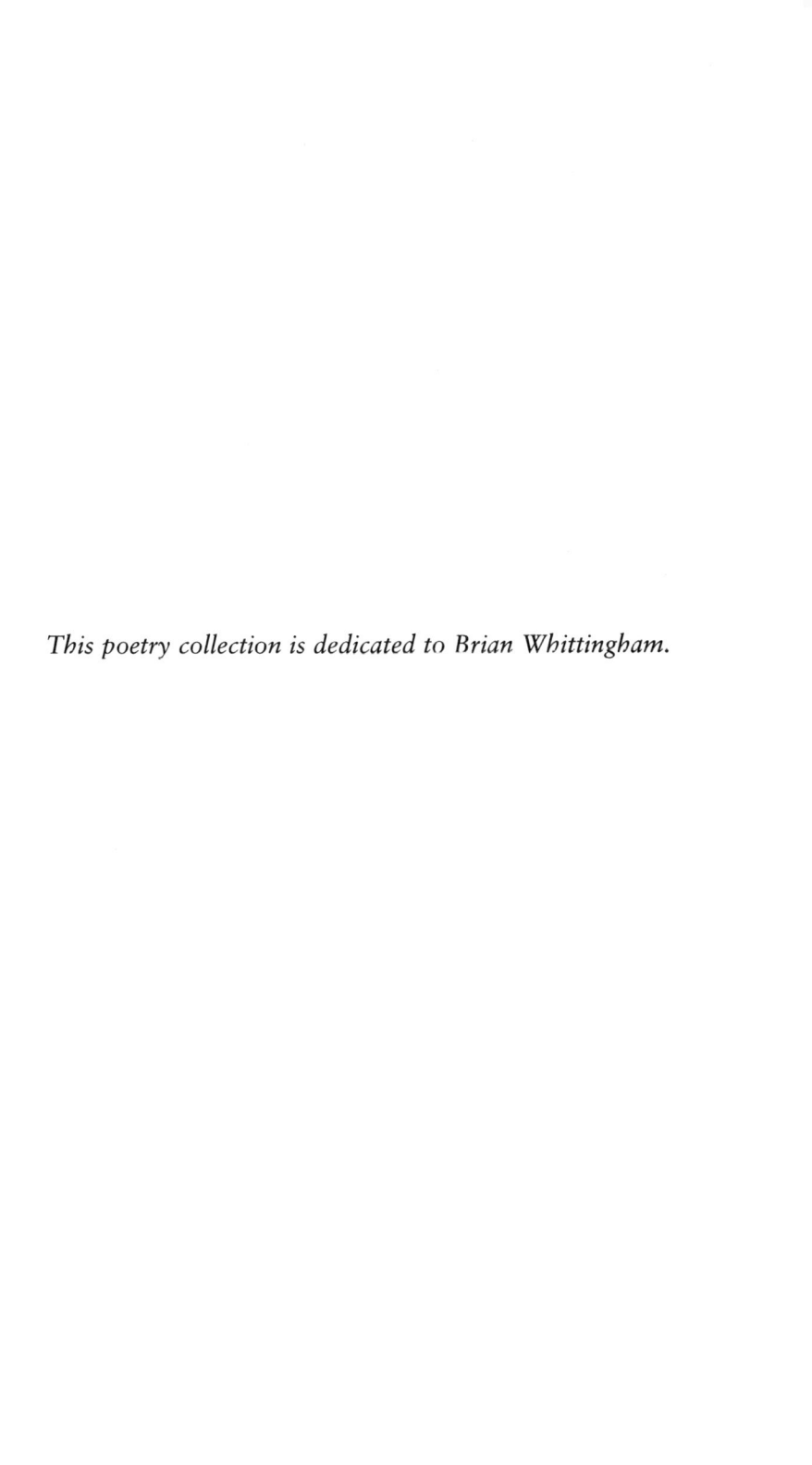

*This poetry collection is dedicated to Brian Whittingham.*

Some poems in this book were previously published in the following:
Strata, The Keith Wright Memorial Magazine,
Preston Polytechnic Poetry Magazine, West Coast Magazine,
Bloody Write publications, Nerve, Cutting Teeth, Chapman,
The Dark Horse, Markings, Poetry Scotland, Skinklin Star,
Deliberately Thirsty, Poésie International, Poetrymagazine.com,
Times Webzine, The Macmillan Book of Scottish Poetry, and
Edinburgh, an Intimate City.

# Contents

| | |
|---|---|
| Introduction: Brian Whittingham | 1 |
| In hope of a happy postman: Des Dillon | 3 |
| Picking Brambles | 7 |
| Coatbridge | 8 |
| Cairnhill | 9 |
| Leningrad | 10 |
| The Wasted Straying | 12 |
| Noiseless Worlds | 14 |
| Days Like These | 15 |
| Sniz | 16 |
| Unrequited Love | 17 |
| Partick Station | 18 |
| Burnt Car | 19 |
| My Dad Had | 21 |
| A Philosophy Of Snow | 22 |
| Monday Book | 23 |
| The Poet Smoking | 24 |
| Rainbows | 25 |
| Photograbbery | 26 |
| Pylons | 27 |
| Christmas Orange | 28 |
| Rain | 29 |
| Sex Education | 30 |
| Turkey | 31 |
| Séance | 32 |
| Football And Famine | 33 |
| Arranmore | 34 |
| Patrick The Survivor | 36 |
| Noreen Boyle's Beach | 38 |
| The Haiku | 39 |

| | |
|---|---|
| Paddy | 40 |
| Politicians | 41 |
| Cucuruzzu | 42 |
| Italian Marigolds | 43 |
| Piazza | 44 |
| Siesta | 45 |
| Afternoon | 46 |
| Old Woman | 47 |
| The Rosary Bell | 48 |
| Technological Revolution | 49 |
| Bones | 50 |
| Cucuruzzu Night | 52 |
| The Sorrow Of The Glory | 53 |
| Change At Preston | 55 |
| Glasgow Chamber Orchestra | 63 |
| Andrew Sinclair in Nunraw | 64 |
| School Trip | 65 |
| Fruit For Sale | 66 |
| Schoolchildren | 67 |
| Someone Else's Tune | 68 |
| Being | 69 |
| Bin Lids And Bits Of Bread | 70 |
| Crisp Bags | 71 |
| Edinburgh Waft | 72 |
| Falling | 73 |
| Garlieston | 74 |
| Olive Groves In Rhodes | 75 |
| Road Signs | 76 |
| These Birds | 77 |
| What Do You See Out Yonder? | 78 |
| Wilderness Of A Leaf | 79 |

# Introduction

I WAS FIRST INTRODUCED to Des Dillon at a book-launch in a long gone Glasgow bookshop called Hatchards. My recollection is of a guy in a long coat who was rather quiet. At this point, the cliché 'Never judge a book by its cover' comes to mind.

Des subsequently attended my *Crazy Day* writing group for a short time. I was living in a flat in Glasgow's West End trying to give my soul and sanity some breathing space when one autumn day Des appeared at the door with someone he introduced to me as Davie-Doom. The conversation roamed (like Des's poetry) from concrete to abstract, from specifics to generalities, and was always engaging and full of Davie-Doom type references. I admit to feeling slightly uneasy about these people who I didn't know too well as their homespun Coatbridge philosophy and the sharp-end imagery of their language filled my cosy bedsit.

Nowadays, to spend an hour in Dillon's company and listen to his quick-fire verbal delivery is to sample the undiluted language of the man that is the raw material used in the crafting of his writing. In computer terminology Dillon is a WYSIWYG person (What You See Is What You Get). No airs and graces and no fancy lah-de-dahs, though in Dillon's case it's worth remembering, moving waters run deep.

After many successes with novels etc. he's finally pulled together a collection of poetry that takes in his impressions of aspects of his life's journey up till now. As these poems have been written over many years they reflect the various voices, moods, writing styles and thought processes that change within any writer over a lengthy period of time. Concrete imagery is mixed with metaphorical abstraction, the specifics of the human condition are mixed with the generalities of emotions that we all engage on an everyday basis, and complex thought processes are mixed with simple straightforward observations.

To read this collection is to share the poet's take on life and to share a passion for language that reflects the human spirit within us all. The Davie-Doom style reference is constantly there and reminds the reader that this is a very individual voice that speaks to us throughout this delightful journey.

I hope Davie-Doom, wherever he is today, is doing well in spirit and that his sidekick of that long gone autumn day, Des Dillon, continues to nurture the poetry in his soul and share it with the rest of us for many years to come.

*Brian Whittingham*

# In hope of a happy postman

I ALWAYS CONSIDERED MYSELF to be first and foremost, a poet. Unfortunately nobody else did. The further away from poetry I moved the more successful I became as a writer. I remember Brian Whittingham telling me he'd feel as if he'd made it as a writer if he could get a collection of short stories published. I'd always felt publishing a collection of poems was success. The grass is always greener right enough.

This collection for me is the pinnacle of my writing career. Simply because it is my belief that poetry is at the cutting edge of language. Out there breaking new ground in the creation of meaning. When I turned to writing prose I never had to wait for a metaphor or simile. The years of writing poetry meant that I was away with a speed and fluidity impossible in poetry. I suppose the best thing to do now is tell you how I came to write poetry.

Although I wrote wee poems at primary school about frolicking lambs and babbling brooks, I started writing seriously when I was eighteen. Mainly influenced by Meat Loaf, Bob Dylan, Coatbridge patter and Fleetwood Mac. I had read a lot of fairy tales and nursery rhymes when I was young which lends my writing the chance of achieving universal depth. My reading was bolstered by comics and the great storytelling tradition that exists in Coatbridge. William Empson said that it is the job of the poet to put the feeling inside the poet's head inside the reader's head. I firmly agree with that. A great storyteller makes use of many of the same tools a poet does, manipulating language in real time to gain and keep the full attention of the audience, so that he can move them mentally, emotionally and spiritually. When I was young I could hold my own in the pubs with the crack. But my attempts at writing then – with a few exceptions – led to some really awful stuff. That was because I was tying to *write* rather than *tell* the story or express *the feeling* honestly. Sometimes the worst thing a writer can do is write.

Then came an event which was, eventually, to change my life. I was twenty-one and into running marathons, kick-boxing and fitness. I had a friend who was a professional boxer and we would train together. One day he passed my gate (I was unemployed) and I asked where he was going. He was going to college to sit Highers in the hope of becoming a PE teacher. At that time, obsessed as I was with physical fitness, a job as a PE teacher was a dream. I found out three Highers were needed for the Jordanhill course and enrolled in Coatbridge Tech the next day. As time passed Peter Nicholson, the English lecturer, suggested that perhaps I should go to Uni and study English Literature. The strange thing was that up to that point I never equated the English course with the writing I was doing at home. The two things were entirely separate in my mind, one being that other rather genteel world of Literature and the other coming directly with my interaction with Coatbrigands and Popular Culture. The thought of associating with that genteel culture was frightening and inviting at the same time. A terrible beauty.

I wrote 'Coatbridge' at that time; influenced by my own cultural background and the English Higher. My writing life since then has involved absorbing elements from both these cultures and using them to express meaning in all the forms I work in. I have come to the conclusion that neither culture should have precedence over the other although politically one does. But each is equally rich and the only barrier to our enjoying what we want to is elitism.

I needed three Bs to get into Strathclyde Uni and I got an A for English a B for Physics and a C for Chemistry. Hardly a high flying academic but I was in. On the form for the BA I simply wrote that I wanted to study poetry. They wrote back and said the structure of the degree required me to pick five subjects. I wrote back saying no thanks I only want to study poetry. They called me in and explained. Did I detect giggling? Thus I was flung into the world of academia, educated with a different knowledge; ill equipped, thinking Plato was a Spanish waiter. My marks were always average but I eventually left with an honours degree. The one thing I did well was writing poetry. Every year I was a prize-winner in the Keith Wright Memorial Poetry Competition. It might mean nothing to you but for me it was a rush seeing my poetry published. That and the encouragement of David Jago, an English lecturer, drove me on. I also got the poem *Coatbridge* published in *Strata* in 1984. The fact that Alasdair Gray, Alan Bold and John Maley were in that wee pamphlet made me think I had made it. If I had known it would be ten years before I'd get anything else published I might have given up. But writers live in hope of a happy postman.

The next time I was to be published was in *West Coast Magazine*, then edited by Brian Whittingham and Joe Murray. It was around 1993 and things were not going well on the writing front. I was teaching English and beginning to think that maybe I didn't have what it took to be a writer. I decided one last push was needed then I would give up. I can't remember how I knew about it but I joined Brian's *Crazy Day* writers' group in Maryhill and learned a lot in a very short time. Brian liked my work and published three poems in *West Coast*. 'Picking Brambles', 'Sniz' and 'Unrequited Love'. Without that encouragement I think I might have given up. That's why this collection is dedicated to him. My writers' group in Castlemilk became legendary at one time but all I did was copy the exact form Brian used in his groups. That honest criticism and lack of pretence sided with solid encouragement led me to where I am and

I in turn passed that on. I could list ten successful contemporary Scottish writers who have a direct link to Brian's workshop or his workshop technique.

After *Crazy Day*, I started a group called *Bloody Write*. We got T-shirts printed with big gothic splodges of blood on them and gatecrashed poetry readings, making a name of some sort but at least getting noticed. *Bloody Write* lives on in cyberspace administered by Kenny Sheerin, a founder member of the original group.

By the time my first novel came out I had written at least a thousand poems. That is a thousand poems I considered to be worth keeping (although others might not). This collection was whittled down from that thousand to about two hundred and sent to Brian W. to edit. He then whittled them down to what you see here. With two exceptions. 'Change at Preston' is responsible for this collection coming into being. I read it at the Edinburgh Book Festival two years ago and Gavin MacDougall was there. He in turn enquired if I had ever published a collection of poetry and if not would I like to? Would I like to!? Too bloody right! Thus 'Change at Preston' is included. The only poem in the collection that Brian didn't pick and I did is 'Schoolchildren'. I include it because it has that special blend of image and metaphor mixed with a universality informed by fairy tales. It seems to represent for me where I have settled as a poet, with a healthy respect for the Literatures at both sides of the cultural divide. I am of course indebted to Brian not just for his work on this selection but his help and encouragement to me and a host of writers this past ten years.

*Des Dillon*
January 2003

# Picking Brambles

Picking brambles;
sunshine wilting
on late September shoulders.
Remember the burns and rivers
rubbing water on the browning backs
of me and Stevie Gallagher.

The rain falls
like a curtain call.
Sun ships between clouds
and the rainbow roars its encore
to a world that is forever moving on
and leaving Stevie Gallagher
splashing in moving memory.
And me?
I'm picking brambles all the while.

# Coatbridge

From this slag hill
this town is mine for 360 degrees.
Straights and spirals, multi-colour light,
fused into white as I spin
on this white hill, on the night.
Coatbridge rides its hills and glens
like some drunken Exocet.
I don't see in my eyes a street
or in this mind a square,
on which I have not stood,
walked, violently run to, cowered from
or staggered through teamed up.
On a cloudless night like tonight
my town, dances with the sky.
My mind drifts through the blanket of light,
like a plane through cloud.
Now;
there are no colours for the grey folk,
and doleful children can't eat fancy lights,
and drunken knives wait, whispering wasp like in the shades,
while Buckfast and blood are flowers to old glades.

I breathe now.
I sigh.
Hunch this young back.
Shovel hands in rustling pockets.
Eyes on everything,
tears in my heart,
I descend through the lights
to the valley
below.

# Cairnhill

Wind blasts a high cairn on the whistling hill,
*Where once in a time,* she said, *an iron
age village tucked itself in the turf.*
A village where ancient men heard even
the drop of a pebble in the night stream;
lit only through clouds by an unsure moon.
She found once, a rusted spearhead buried
in a cage of ribs. I deduced that peace
and war are not a modern trait, while she,
being an archaeologist, informed my obvious
uninformed, ignorance, that the spear,
from those ribs, was respect, placed in the grave;
a religious act to a great man chief.
Nodding insincerely I strolled on
to the bleating hill, up towards the cairn.
Cairnhill was dew shone and peaceful that day.

# Leningrad

I had asked Natasha
one night on the ice
what she thought of.
*Of St Peter and green trees
and life in the deadness of war,*
she whispered.
Leningrad lay cold that Christmas.
This cold had never crawled so far south;
Siberian winds of a hundred years.
In February
a hundred thousand people died.
In March the thaw never came
and a hundred thousand died again.
When the railway was finished
and the food was coming through,
Natasha, my young love in the rye grass,
in the laughing snow,
died.
With the food
and the thaw
Leningrad still died.
The Nazis,
white wolfs in the snow,
waited, and waited.
But the music
would surrender
only tears.
When the ice on the lake melted
I was a boat-builder.
Rations went up into strength and happiness.
The Germans never did come
and the Party announced a Victory of sorts.

The next year
when the snow came
we were ready.

# The Wasted Straying

Mrs. Gallagher still drinks
and punches her man, drunk.
She wrings her sober hands in mourning
for a morning's memory.
Then the dusk slips in
with the cheap wine.

Her sons hustle on the fringes
of the big time,
drug deal in relays,
cringing five yards sharp from the cops.
They don't fight much now,
since the preying knives.

The Autumn sets the big sun
laughing at the primitive landscape
that leapt, fretting, out
the phantom steelworks,
sold now, to Taiwan.
We slant our eyes at the Talisman.

Thomson buys bags of potatoes
at the season's prices,
food of our forefathers.
He wraps them in newspapers
and winters them in his coalbunker,
to dole to dolequeue folk,
for bags more in scarce times.

Once in the corrupt hours
haunts in the lane
I watched the woman from up the block
squeeze her neighbour's son's purity
in a delicate place:
talk through windows
*She was forty-two last month you know.*
A black and white senile telly
still fades out
twilight windows of the Old Folks houses.
The volume is hell menacing
as they adjust the knob to maladapted ears.

Nothing has changed these years gone.
Only the dogs are different.
Black hounds rip at rancid bins
and ooze accused curs' guilty label:
upward eyes, deranged, downward ears,
tail obscenely tucked.

On the walk to Thomson's
I saw a mongrel tongue, hoodwinked
at a bin in distaste,
refused even potato peels; the wasted stray.
The people eat them now, I heard.
The hidden truth in a black bag.

## Noiseless Worlds

Isn't it strange,
how we speak,
with all the little things
that are not noise?

Not words,
but movements,
looks and eyes,
that swallow
the universe;
to convert its vastness
into sadness, and joy
and births, and deaths
of a million moments;
without speaking.

# Days Like These

The day draws the clouds
together in grey rain
that will not go away.

There is a landscape
today of coldness;
and wet trains on distant tracks.

# Sniz

Can you feel me?
My name is pain
and I sniz through your heart
making jigsaws
of every thought and memory
and place you feel or see.

Uncontent with breaking,
I choose not to shatter
but to sniz;
to cut slowly,
sawing and turning,
winding out long, long distances.
Taking my time,
and yours,
inflicting.
And when you're finished,
I leave you all the pieces
to fit back together.

# Unrequited Love

It's like...
you give someone a Christmas gift
and they give you nothing in return;
multiplied by the size of the sun.

So yesterday
I rained for forty days
and cried for other nights.

And tonight,
As Water washes Her tears
on my hair,
in the fizz
from the starlit falls,
I love you still;
multiplied by the moon
in my eyes.

## Partick Station

Eighty odd degrees today.
Partick Station.
The tracks schweep and shimmer,
winding out blinding distances.

A continental mist
heat hazes the University,
leaving all its Gothic pointed bits
in blue skies.

Men and women
slowed in the sun
look each other up and down
in stillness.

Their airs are full of sex,
their graces droop in heat.

She walks in, blond,
tanned tight black dress,
legs coming from the hemline.
All the heads turn.

The guy slumped
on the bench
near me says:

*Its hot enough without the likes of that.*

# Burnt Car

Death to the melted glass
hanging into the windspace
like tongues of heated Perspex.
But raspy as stones on a path.

What's left of the steering wheel
impales itself on its own column.
The seats are dark labyrinths
of black charred springs and things.

The top half of the windscreen
flops itself, as if it jumped,
like a Salvador Dali clock,
over the useless handbrake.

The radio lies dead beside the gearstick,
too cheap to be stolen.
The paint, heated to snowy whiteness
in the boot, is an avalanche.

The windscreen wipers droop,
like snakes' tongues,
onto the body, licking dust
in the worst of droughts.

A front tyre
intact in absurdity;
the wind, last night,
blew in its favour.

The wing mirror popped,
escaping the inferno,
as it roared the chromium
into purples and rainbows.

The number plate is missing,
presumed molten; the silver sick
below the anonymous grin
of the teethy radiator.

# My Dad Had

My Dad had
various crazy traps and weapons
set up and spring loaded with hate
in case THEY tried to get in
through the garden.

My Dad had
nine wanes and forty years of building site
metaphors of concrete and rain
and hard men that never die
but drink their fame away
day after day after day.

My Dad had
them eyes that stared but never saw
what we saw – his two clenched fists
in the middle of summer flowers
and bees buzzing by *Hi* he'd say
in his own demented way.

# A Philosophy of Snow

Micro-angels holding hands
and lonesome, in gliding
rumours and murmurs of
a hypocrisy in snow;
a falling paradise
over a fallen paradise.
Trees of ages,
unclear with snow, brandish
an envy of green branches
that strain under cover,
below and above,
the dizzy eternity
that is



White.

# Monday Book

Crouched in Post Office doorways
away from the rain
and righteous eyes.

I look at her
and she moves
more into less corner,

clutching her son
in one hand and
a wet Monday Book in the other.

Her fear's real
as her wet hair from
relentless cloud after cloud.

The boy, a Tabula Rasa
in a world waiting
to paint him black

and her daily bread
lost in Carlsberg Specials
and king size fags.

# The Poet Smoking

After all
I've given up for life,
the booze
the dope
the acid
the speed
the mushies
the glue
the smack
the shookie
the steroids
the women
the stealing
the fighting
It's the only bit of suicide
I've got left.

# Rainbows

A dancing million
sunbursting raindrops painting
rainbows in the sky.

# Photograbbery

First thing I know
is the flash;
a pint of radioactive milk,
spiked with glitter and sunlight,
thrashes into my face.

She kidnaps me
and the Museum Of Religious Art.
Abducted,
I lie in paper memories
in some
Washington suburb sideboard.
A foreign soul,
photograbbed.

# Pylons

> The
>
> pylons
>
> take up their stance
>
> big fat ladies holding up
>
> their hems
>
> and walking careful not to flash
>
> their reinforced
>
> knickers they
>
> head south where
>
> they might fold their arms and tap
>
> their front foot on an
>
> imaginary border become real

## Christmas Orange

There's always that orange
in the kitchen cupboard,
shining above the tinsel like a bulb,
me on toetips, tight and stretching.

I only rolled it over
                       into
                                  shadows.

Now it's seventy-pence for six.
Spanish fruit for Christmas stockings;
smallest are most juicy.

I roll them over
into shadows

of stockings. They swing
all night like stars
awaiting children.

My Beacon is that Orange memory,
somehow above all
my little Bethlehems.
And I'm delivered now and then
from all anxiety
into the simplicity
of not knowing
where fingertips search.

# Rain

A million sardines
flapping insane on
the wet-velvet tarmac.

## Sex Education

The teacher said:
Don't wear ski pants nor leggings,
they hug the crotch
and young boys get ideas
from tight crotches.

*Isn't that what it's all about?*
thought Lynn Marie.

The teacher said:
Don't wear your trousers
too tight around your organ,
young girls won't know
where to put their eyes.

*Want a fuckin bet?*
thought Lynn Marie.

The teacher said:
Keep to the left in the corridors,
we don't want you all squeezing by.
It's not good for young boys and girls
to be rubbing against each other
in the crush, it makes you aware of things.

*You're fuckin right there!*
thought Lynn Marie.

# Turkey

OK Turkey:
put down the baseball bat,
turn off the Techno,
fold away the knife,
put the jellies back in the bottle,
flush the acid down the pan,
stub out the joint,
cork the Buckie,
spit out that E
get the Cats off,
get yer arse out the five o ones
an get to yer bed,
yer mammy's comin in from the bingo.

# Séance

Someone is near me,
reading unaware
her perfume bubbles in my blood.
The rosy champagne of yesterday

pains like the Bends
in my veins,
frothing to the chambers
of heart and skull;
the great Cathedrals
where love is decompressed and chilled.

I'd thought it safe
until she sat there.
The White Musk
thrust itself in me.
Repossessed by your Ghost
rippling from the pages' turning wake
I rise and walk to the window.

# Football and Famine

Turn on the TV
Packie Bonner's lightning save on one side,
Famine's bug eyed children in Sudan on the other.

On the one hand you're proud to be Irish
On the other you're ashamed to be human.

# Arranmore

From Arranmore
the white houses on the Donegal shore
are wave crest after wave crest
on a motionless pink sea of rock
and a backfall of yellow mountains.
The Gaelic place names tug at tradition.
The big wind tugs at my hair
and buffets the Atlantic breakers
four horses high.

By the pine trees and peaty stream
the clenched wind whispers;
*Eist le mo chrio...*
the language of the land surface –
of the wind, of the peat, of the sea,
of the emigrants, of searchers like me
and the IRA – where are you Mo Chrio?

I strain against
the same wind that suffered
against the faces of those who left.
Whistling wires howl like banshees
for the ruined Church and Fishing Boats
that can't go out and those who did.
A bath towel hanging for ten years
has been bleached and shredded.

The barman in O'Donnell's tells me:
*They show ye pictures of Dublin*
*an a wee splash of water. Nothin equals this –*
his hand follows a breaker home
to me licking the salt on my crusting lips.
I ask of the economy and he tells me:
*A dry pound at home's worth two abroad.*

Unexaggerated fifty foot waves
smash on shoreline rocks.
For those who remained;

who would face a sea like this?
For those who left;
who would face a sea like this?

The west coast is desolate.
There is nobody. There is nothing
from frightening winds to plummeting cliffs
and rocks being patiently shaped
by a sea of cold blue and ice-white foam.

## Patrick the Survivor

November is cold in the Rosses
where Patrick Gallagher held his dead brother afloat
for nineteen hours clinging to the upturned boat.
A woman wanders Aphort Strand for her family
lost from the harvest of the Rutland Channels.
They say she walks Arranmore still – searching.

*We clung to the upturned hull.*
*Every ten yards the boat rolled*
*and another lost their hold.*
*One by one they slipped*
*into the ice-water of November.*
*Every ten yards the boat rolled*
*and another lost their hold.*
*Till only me, my father and brother*
*clung to the turning hull.*
*And on that boat that night*
*I watched the lights of Arranmore*
*go out one by one until – blackness,*
*the roar of the sea, and songs pouring over the waves.*
*My brother thought he was on a train.*
*'I've had nothin to eat since we left Derry,' he said.*
*He looked out the window of his train*
*and seen his station coming in.*
*Every ten yards the boat rolled*
*and another lost their hold.*
*My father, taken by the tide*
*my brother taken at my side.*
*I sang him Irish songs into heaven*
*clinging to his dead weight body*
*like a Siamese twin.*

*I was picked up at Inchgeerath.*
*The folk of Mehgreerach heard shouting*
*in the night but thought it the harvesters*
*home playing drunk at Aphort Strand.*

*And on Wednesday the thirteenth of November,*
*all through the night,*
*figures of rain drenched women*
*and children and men*
*moved against the sky.*
*An absolute still broken by them,*
*the sea*
*and the keening.*
*Arranmore; one big wake house.*
*Rosaries trail from the shawls and veils*
*Of women who pray in Gaelic.*
*Nine bodies buried in one grave.*
*The island turned and prayed at the sea*
*to give up the lost bodies.*
*One day they will all come home.*

Arranmore. So silent; but the sea.

## Noreen Boyle's Beach

So where are you now Noreen Boyle?
You wanted poetry but stayed away
from this Looking. On this beach

the pebbles are clacking like pool balls
under the waves' Hotpoint number four soap-sud wash.
The gulls are squadrons of squeaky flies
hanging around a light-bulb sun, yellow,
through a mad emulsion of grey clouds.

It's all old rope and scrubbing brushes.
Two magpies fly by, cruising like children;
there is nothing shining on the tan linoleum of sand,
nor hidden in the skirting boards of concrete and rock.
The sea will Brillo-Pad these to dust
and the ropes will fray on wave frills
and the scrubbing brushes float away,
bristles upwards, trying to polish
the day to soap-powder blue
and the glossy night to stars
that one by one come in
and one by one
go out.

# The Haiku

It's the gap between the first two lines
and the last line
that forces the reader to create an image
in a mental

leap.

A good writer will force the reader
to make the image he wants.
It's like jumping the burn.
A good writer will make sure you jump
at a certain bit – the careless writer
will have hundreds
jumping any old where.

# Paddy

You arty bastards
that like to paddle in insanity
should see the twenty eight stone schizoid
that used to be
Big Paddy McGhee.
That would push your socks
and shoes back on.

# Politicians

They are tight-walking
the fragile ice of lies and power;
spouting promises
which are like ice because
the breath that makes them
melts them.

## Cucuruzzu

From the Franciscan house in Cucuruzzu
Monte Cassino perches like a vulture
on the wind of empty days and Monks
walking twenty lonely long corridors;
measuring out the last of monastic peace.

It's stony and obstinate as pyramids.
These Benedictines used to be on the trail of peace –
trailing us behind and us ignorant to what they prayed
for.
But

now

our might of fast cars buzzing
like flies on a carcass
are too heavy to pull.

The stars are moving on and out while we wait
in a stagnant pool of space where no-one
will hear us scream and no-one will see His Face.

## Italian Marigolds

Two little girls with marigolds
pressed against their breast.

The sun shinning on the rustic houses
and, high on the hill the church bell rings the Angelus.

Squinting in the sun, they smile up;
their eyes narrow and blessed.

The mountains rise up;
behind them, blue skies.

*Buongiorno* they say in small voices
not shy nor afraid. *Buongiorno* I say.

They return to orange petals;
I to my work and in the hazy distance

a man cobbles off on a lazy horse
going nowhere in particular.

Two old men lace the sky above their black hats
with warm smoke from slow pipes.

Cucuruzzu settles for afternoon sun.

## Piazza

Resting in the warm calm of sun.
A full throated Italian motorbike
surfaces in the square,
filling old stones with new roars.
It gets close to my comfort
then turns and fades outwards –
like I'm in still waters
and a dangerous fish stalks the deep.
But in the end it's peace and sweet Italian voices
falling on this unfamiliar pillow.

## Siesta

An old man meanders by
dressed for a Scottish winter.
The sun glints off the wine bottle
he grasps with monkey fingers.
Loose in his left hand, six eggs.

He comes back unchanged
two hours later except for
the empty wine bottle and
the breeze in the fingers of his left hand,
the shadow of his cap on his forehead

and the group on Cucuruzzu square
has changed position but the same talk
whistles over the top of the slow swing of the bottle.

# Afternoon

The sun in the mist –
red – sharp edges you can
look at and ragged mountains.

A woman bent over in a field –
a gigantic bull with mud Wellingtons
chews away at some vines.

An old man with a black hat
lights a cigarette like it's the first and the last
trail of smoke he'll blow up the purple sky

where stars are pushing
their light against the sunset.
It will always go and they will always come back.

You can tell the terraced fields and dry plants
are bursting with the pressure of spring
pushing down from the red sun.

Morning will bring inversions along the valley
and pushing up from the roots, rucks and rivers,
a distant thunder underground drumming out a rhythm
we have forgotten but can't forget.

# Old Woman

An old woman gathering sheaves of sticks.
They crackle in the same pitch they'll burn.
Her voice sings across the sunlit fields
expecting no answer.
I smile and she struggles
unsure with her sticks.

# The Rosary Bell

The rosary bell
brings a stream of old women
in black along the ribbon of white dusty road.

Each are a walking Hail-Mary,
Our Father or Glory Be.
I can't tell if it's the prayers

or the walk or the bell that brought them
from cold shuttered rooms
and mosquito nets in spring.

They pass the giggling
jeans-factory girls like planets
in the wrong solar system.

They will float like virgins
into the endless space of religion
and silence might never touch them.

A factory girl gazes at the hills.

# Technological Revolution

The Cucuruzzu cocks
move round the square with the sun.
Children kick away at a ball
and an old woman,
squinting,
feeds her chickens.

Houses hold the rocky hill
in the most unimaginable fashion
and people drive goats and donkeys onwards –
missed by the shrapnel
of technological revolution.

The people travel slowly though,
for them, it's only early spring
and in and out them swallows
knit the invisible threads of summer.

The roads from the snowy mountains
wind winter downhill into summer.
Cars that hang with rosary beads
head miraculously at each other
on spaghetti roads. They always miss
and the beads click the windscreen
with the ABS brakes.

# Bones

The Word from the streets
is the stalking cats that can almost talk
and the click of sticks being sorted
for fires like the bones of ancestors.
Bones that this village and all men
picked to reach today.
There will always be bones
and fire will always be master

in winter villages and summer fields.
In Gargliano Valley the river has stopped.
Its reflection pins old women
to the shady walls of houses.
And, with their hands fumbling behind backs
they gossip about the sky, the river, the holy church,
the poet high on the wall. Then
they stop gathering what is new

and not known in the nets
of what the whole village knows
and in the sweet smell of burning wood
they wave children up the winding alleys
to waiting dinners, big fat mammas
and yammering cats.
The men walk in funeral procession
for the piazza's important work is done.

The iron hammer in the cappella clock tower hammers
out the message that time is God's.
But their Gargliano shuffle
will have none of the knocking bell.
The old men and women step out a rhythm
older than iron; slower than time.
Through them the children buzz
like summer bees in a poppy field
blown by a warm but gentle breeze.
At supper time dinners are passed
from house to house like Christmas gifts.

## Cucuruzzu Night

There's a crescent moon.
The night is falling on the valley
and the mountains are being erased by mist.
Cats push through dust like little road sweepers,
their engine purrs drive through layers
of cherry blossoms rocking
in the light of artificial lamps.

Soon the mountains will be black shapes against stars
and dark ridged hills spattered with distant lights.

A dog barks who knows how far away.
A lamb bleats. A pretty young girl
closes the window shutters and a woman's
heels click out across the square.

A cock will crow in the morning.
But for now any point of light will do
to believe there are others out there

looking too.

# The Sorrow of the Glory

Monte Cassino. Walking the cloisters
in the vanishing steps of St Benedict,
in shattered fragments of pillars and stone
rebuilt from the ashes of war.
And stepping from the hot white
of the dusty cloisters the chapel
resurrects through the darkness
that is in my eyes because the light
outside was too bright to see.

The simple story repaints itself
on the roof and the high dome
pointing to God. The painted Word falls
through the enormous ornament of church
and drifts on the melancholy voices of monks
chanting out the Sorrow of the Glory.

Somehow simple melodies laid live
over an imperceptible moan of organ
conjures more God than the bashful
of Angels and trumpet blowing alabaster boys.
This chapel is a love letter to God.
The Words are curly metals and gold leaf plaster.
The sentences, flat expanses of intricate marble.

There is a confusion that can't be fathomed
in the hush of foreign whispers,
the rush of shapes and colours
and the Word through an Italian microphone
crackling like little lightning bolts
off the hard unrelenting walls.

There is one light that shines always in the sanctuary
and a simple melody that laces clouds on my feet
and carries me at the head of the procession
of my life – I turn and looking back – oh
how many candles I have lit
from the one solitary light.
And so, blessed in the smoky breath
of incense I turn and walk out
into the light outside that blinds.

# Change at Preston

Engine tugging
High on Glasgow
Central Station
Silver raining
River bridges
Southward flying
South west Glasgow
Blantyre passing
Craig all empty
Children hungry
Fathers angry
Shops all empty
Crows on cornfields
Mental inmates
Carstairs Junction
Mist on Tinto
Young girl flirting
Must remember
change at Preston

Southern Uplands
Trees all waving
Sheep in green fields
Trees all wispy
Just like Ireland
Someone's paper
Over river
Provo's peacemaker
Main line bending
Cars all passing
Loyal uproar
Under bridges
Orange and gleaming
In through valleys
Raindrops falling
Service station
Round by hillsides
Must remember
change at Preston

Moorlands marshy
Ecclefechan
Clouds are rolling
Pylons standing
Cables stranding
Road above us
Fast train passing
Pass like rockets
Free range chickens
Road below us
Concrete bridges
Rock perched castle
On the border
Goodbye Scotland
Inter-City
Pass like rockets
Stopped at station
Must remember
change at Preston

Carlisle station
Metal railings
Liverpudlians
Open windows
Five yobs drinking
Red brick houses
Screaming shouting
Little hamlet
Buzz of talking
Curly blond girl
Train gets noisy
Brown eyes swivel
Sexual contact
Out the window
Snub nosed horses
Penrith passing
Fields all folding
Pass like rockets
Must remember
change at Preston

Mirror window
Eyebrows raising
Through the tunnel
Caught her staring
Good reflection
Clouds all soaring
She's so lovely
Hills all raising
Brown eyes swivel
Pass like rockets
Wordsworth country
Rivers running
Under bridges
Pass like rockets
Sunshine breaking
Secret smiling
Kendal passing
Mona Lisa
Must remember
change at Preston

Train wheels slowing
Heads all swinging
Blond bird leaving
Engine stopping
Wagons shunting
Someone waiting
Blond bird kissing
Heart is sinking
Engine inching
Blond head turning
Goodbye flirting
My mouth smiling
Brown eye winking
Train gets moving
Lost forever
Perfect beauty
Sheep all huddling
Pass like rockets
Must remember
change at Preston

Cars all pointing
One direction
Derelict station
Stacked up train stock
Coastline shining
Radiation
Pass like rockets
Seascale looming
Windscale whispers
Seashore lapping
Sunshine setting
Horses chewing
No more flirting
Golfers golfing
Council housing
Massive river
In Lancaster
Zones of colour
Must remember
change at Preston

Train gets moving
Landscape gardens
Four girls smiling
Pass like rockets
Fields all furrowed
Small roads winding
Smoking hamlet
Sky gets darker
Signposts pointing
No-one watching
Night-time falling
Darkness coming
Fear is crowding
Faces peering
In reflection
Got me covered
Paranoia
Eye-lids closing
Must remember
change at Preston
change at Preston
change at Preston
change at Preston

Wake from dreaming
Eyes unfocussed
Brain cells guessing
Well past Preston

# Glasgow Chamber Orchestra

*(Concerto For Flute And Orchestra Jaques Ibert, 1890-1962)*

The flute valves
opening and shutting,
clumping like little
frog mouths
among the songs of birds.

Through shoals of violins
twisting in the light
the Cello player swims
in and out
like a dolphin
moving
in her own clear waters
free and blue.

# Andrew Sinclair in Nunraw

This holy night
Andrew's in the field
scaring the cows.
Woooo he goes Whoooo
and off the cows run
to the light of the moon.

But the bull turns and snorts –
steam cleaning the grass
to the clean heels Andrew shows
making for the safety of the fence.

He stood on the gate-post laughing
at me laughing at him
and the moon silver in his hair.

# School Trip

Leaving Dover
the gulls are following
the wide foam motorway
laid by the ferry throbbing south.

It's just like the children in Stirling
who followed the invisible ribbons
of laughter when the bus left
until their parents' reflections slid
window by window and faded
in the folding waves of children.

The same children
will buzz behind
their own disappearing childhood.
But, for now, their naïve velocity
knows no estimation
of acceleration.

## Fruit for Sale

There's fruit Te Koop
all along the Dutch borderline.
And the kids give more thought
to the apple's surface
than to the dead Americans
in their thousands
under foreign earth surfaces
where they shall never bear
their intended fruit.

And I hope the stars
may stripe the sky tonight
and in the morning,
a blue sky
and a red sunrise
like an apple thrown up
in victory.

# Schoolchildren

Twilight,
all your unshamed eyes
are crinkled sweet papers,
paired and purple.
Easy stars sprinkle
faces with glitter
over warm gasps for joy.
In the forest
we see fairies for fire-flies,
wolves for shadows,
giants for branches.
And in the distance,

an apple,

hangs between us
and a lonesome moon,

shining

for passing children.

# Someone Else's Tune

The bow is a bar
of ice melting on the
warm strings
of bass and violins,
dripping the notes
into the air,
humid
with the joys
and tears
and little fears
that dance for now
to someone else's tune.

# Being

Sometimes, when I look out at the stars
This feeling rises in my belly and I laugh.
And all my troubles fade away.
And the world's troubles fade away.
Just for that moment,
When my mouth is open
And the dogs are barking in the sand,
I am perfectly balanced
On the absolute grace of being.

## Bin Lids and Bits of Bread

When you're young
and trying to catch a bird
you're trying to catch your own spirit
with bin lids and bits of bread.

And every time you catch
A Blackbird or Thrush
You move on to
More exotic birds
So that you're always
Moving on,
Always moving up,
Chasing your own spirit.

# Crisp Bags

On this new and windy day
Crisp bags scoop up the morning.
They will land in late afternoon
Where stillness will hear their last scratches.

Above them on the telephone wires
The house martins, swallows and swifts chirp
And sing out telephone numbers and messages
And little love stories passing through their feet.

But on the poles, on the roofs, in the trees,
Crows crouch waiting to spread bad news.
The crisp bags lift and empty a new wind
Into the early evening sun going down

And down.

The twitch and lift of a crow's wing.

# Edinburgh Waft

There's something about that day.
It wasn't her lace shirt flapping
or her pre-Raphaelite
red hair
tearing
down.

or

the fact that she
held Edinburgh's eye among
bungee jumpers and birling jesters

or

the way she spun
her shawl following
the drum beats down
a thousand years

or

the winds of passing buses
flinging her hair into strange
looks of passers by

or

jugglers spinning
sticks of fire reflected
in her eyes

it was when she
held my trembling
eye in her ghostly stare.

# Falling

Sometimes in my bed
I feel the walls fall away.
I fall into darkness
and keep falling
through the streets
through the town
through the fields
through the forest
and keep falling
so that everything's becoming colder.
Darker.

# Garlieston

Driving between Garlieston and Whithorn
I seen a wide wingspanned hawk
Hovering and flying along the road.
I slowed to watch it, took a bend
And there was a young deer standing,
It's new antlers jewelled with rain.
It walked some trembling steps
Looking for a way back to the woods.
That's when I knew
I had finally left the city.

# Olive Groves in Rhodes

As we pass in the last bus to Falaraki
packed with tourists
in the fields
old women in black
pick olives and press them
till their green skin
bursts
and oil oozes.
We're squeezed
together like olives.
I feel your body
as sweet and spicy
as extra virgin olive oil
and long to touch,
to squeeze.

# Road Signs

Today the road signs
take on new significance.
Forty with red circles round them
celebrate my birthday
all along this Galloway road.

The tide's in as if
it couldn't come in any further.
What will it be like when
I'm bombing along hitting seventy
on some narrowing road
with the dark water of forever
on each side,
lapping at the tar?

# These Birds

These birds describe the figure six in the air.
Focused just beneath the surface,
the waves projecting
the corrugated shapes of fish.

Then they crash into the water
like Spitfires shot down.

Obliterated.

But they rise
and sometimes with the prize
of a fish
uncorrugated
swinging from their beak.

How many times have you dived
for love or lust or wealth?
Failed and lay flaccid
On the sea of poor me's?

But these birds
they rise every time
and describe their figure six
and

plummet

and surge

and surface

and fly

# What Do You See Out Yonder?

What do you see out yonder?
I see the sea and nothing else.
Keep looking – keep looking.
I see the sea, the sky and shore
And nothing else – nothing more.
Keep looking – keep looking.

# Wilderness of a Leaf

The world's whatever size you want it to be –
claustrophobia in New York
or a child's gaze wandering
the wilderness of a leaf.

# Some other books published by **LUATH** PRESS

## THE QUEST FOR

**The Quest for the Celtic Key**
Karen Ralls-MacLeod and
Ian Robertson
ISBN 0 946487 73 1  HB  £18.99

**The Quest for Arthur**
Stuart McHardy
ISBN 1 842820 12 5  HB  £16.99

## POLITICS & CURRENT ISSUES

**Scotlands of the Mind**
Angus Calder
ISBN 1 84282 008 7  PB  £9.99

**Trident on Trial: the case for people's disarmament**
Angie Zelter
ISBN 1 84282 004 4  PB  £9.99

**Uncomfortably Numb: A Prison Requiem**
Maureen Maguire
ISBN 1 84282 001 X  PB  £8.99

**Scotland: Land & Power – Agenda for Land Reform**
Andy Wightman
ISBN 0 946487 70 7  PB  £5.00

**Old Scotland New Scotland**
Jeff Fallow
ISBN 0 946487 40 5  PB  £6.99

**Some Assembly Required: Scottish Parliament**
David Shepherd
ISBN 0 946487 84 7  PB  £7.99

**Notes from the North**
Emma Wood
ISBN 0 946487 46 4  PB  £8.99

## NATURAL WORLD

**The Hydro Boys: pioneers of renewable energy**
Emma Wood
ISBN 1 84282 016 8  HB  £16.99

**Wild Scotland**
James McCarthy
ISBN 0 946487 37 5  PB  £7.50

**Wild Lives: Otters – On the Swirl of the Tide**
Bridget MacCaskill
ISBN 0 946487 67 7  PB  £9.99

**Wild Lives: Foxes – The Blood is Wild**
Bridget MacCaskill
ISBN 0 946487 71 5  PB  £9.99

**Scotland – Land & People: An Inhabited Solitude**
James McCarthy
ISBN 0 946487 57 X  PB  £7.99

**The Highland Geology Trail**
John L Roberts
ISBN 0 946487 36 7  PB  £4.99

**'Nothing but Heather!'**
Gerry Cambridge
ISBN 0 946487 49 9  PB  £15.00

**Red Sky at Night**
John Barrington
ISBN 0 946487 60 X  PB  £8.99

**Listen to the Trees**
Don MacCaskill
ISBN 0 946487 65 0  PB  £9.99

## ISLANDS

**The Islands that Roofed the World: Easdale, Belnahua, Luing & Seil:**
Mary Withall
ISBN 0 946487 76 6  PB  £4.99

**Rum: Nature's Island**
Magnus Magnusson
ISBN 0 946487 32 4  PB  £7.95

## LUATH GUIDES TO SCOTLAND

**The North West Highlands: Roads to the Isles**
Tom Atkinson
ISBN 0 946487 54 5  PB  £4.95

**Mull and Iona: Highways and Byways**
Peter Macnab
ISBN 0 946487 58 8   PB   £4.95

**The Northern Highlands: The Empty Lands**
Tom Atkinson
ISBN 0 946487 55 3   PB   £4.95

**The West Highlands: The Lonely Lands**
Tom Atkinson
ISBN 0 946487 56 1   PB   £4.95

**South West Scotland**
Tom Atkinson
ISBN 0 946487 04 9   PB   £4.95

## TRAVEL & LEISURE

**Die Kleine Schottlandfibel [Scotland Guide in German]**
Hans-Walter Arends
ISBN 0 946487 89 8   PB   £8.99

**Let's Explore Edinburgh Old Town**
Anne Bruce English
ISBN 0 946487 98 7   PB   £4.99

**Edinburgh's Historic Mile**
Duncan Priddle
ISBN 0 946487 97 9   PB   £2.99

**Pilgrims in the Rough: St Andrews beyond the 19th hole**
Michael Tobert
ISBN 0 946487 74 X   PB   £7.99

## FOOD & DRINK

**The Whisky Muse: Scotch whisky in poem & song**
various, ed. Robin Laing
ISBN 0 946487 95 2   PB   £12.99

**First Foods Fast: good simple baby meals**
Lara Boyd
ISBN 1 84282 002 8   PB   £4.99

**Edinburgh and Leith Pub Guide**
Stuart McHardy
ISBN 0 946487 80 4   PB   £4.95

## WALK WITH LUATH

**Skye 360: walking the coastline of Skye**
Andrew Dempster
ISBN 0 946487 85 5   PB   £8.99

**Walks in the Cairngorms**
Ernest Cross
ISBN 0 946487 09 X   PB   £4.95

**Short Walks in the Cairngorms**
Ernest Cross
ISBN 0 946487 23 5   PB   £4.95

**The Joy of Hillwalking**
Ralph Storer
ISBN 0 946487 28 6   PB   £7.50

**Scotland's Mountains before the Mountaineers**
Ian R Mitchell
ISBN 0 946487 39 1   PB   £9.99

**Mountain Days and Bothy Nights**
Dave Brown and Ian R Mitchell
ISBN 0 946487 15 4   PB   £7.50

## SPORT

**Ski & Snowboard Scotland**
Hilary Parke
ISBN 0 946487 35 9   PB   £6.99

**Over the Top with the Tartan Army**
Andy McArthur
ISBN 0 946487 45 6   PB   £7.99

## BIOGRAPHY

**The Last Lighthouse**
Sharma Krauskopf
ISBN 0 946487 96 0   PB   £7.99

**Tobermory Teuchter**
Peter Macnab
ISBN 0 946487 41 3   PB   £7.99

**Bare Feet and Tackety Boots**
Archie Cameron
ISBN 0 946487 17 0   PB   £7.95

**Come Dungeons Dark**
John Taylor Caldwell
ISBN 0 946487 19 7   PB   £6.95

## HISTORY

**Civil Warrior**
Robin Bell
ISBN 1 84282 013 3  HB  £10.99

**A Passion for Scotland**
David R Ross
ISBN 1 84282 019 2  PB  £5.99

**Reportage Scotland**
Louise Yeoman
ISBN 0 946487 61 8  PB  £9.99

**Blind Harry's Wallace**
Hamilton of Gilbert-
ISBN 0 946487 33 2  PB  £8.99

**Blind Harry's Wallace**
field [intro/ed Elspeth King]
ISBN 0 946487 43 X  HB  £15.00

## SOCIAL HISTORY

**Pumpherston: the story of a shale oil village**
Sybil Cavanagh
ISBN 1 84282 011 7  HB  £17.99

**Pumpherston: the story of a shale oil village**
Sybil Cavanagh
ISBN 1 84282 015 X  PB  £7.99

**Shale Voices**
Alistair Findlay
ISBN 0 946487 78 2  HB  £17.99

**Shale Voices**
Alistair Findlay
ISBN 0 946487 63 4  PB  £10.99

**A Word for Scotland**
Jack Campbell
ISBN 0 946487 48 0  PB  £12.99

## ON THE TRAIL OF

**On the Trail of William Wallace**
David R Ross
ISBN 0 946487 47 2  PB  £7.99

**On the Trail of Robert the Bruce**
David R Ross
ISBN 0 946487 52 9  PB  £7.99

**On the Trail of Mary Queen of Scots**
J Keith Cheetham
ISBN 0 946487 50 2  PB  £7.99

**On the Trail of Bonnie Prince Charlie**
David R Ross
ISBN 0 946487 68 5  PB  £7.99

**On the Trail of Robert Burns**
John Cairney
ISBN 0 946487 51 0  PB  £7.99

**On the Trail of John Muir**
Cherry Good
ISBN 0 946487 62 6  PB  £7.99

**On the Trail of Queen Victoria in the Highlands**
Ian R Mitchell
ISBN 0 946487 79 0  PB  £7.99

**On the Trail of Robert Service**
G Wallace Lockhart
ISBN 0 946487 24 3  PB  £7.99

**On the Trail of the Pilgrim Fathers**
J Keith Cheetham
ISBN 0 946487 83 9  PB  £7.99

## FOLKLORE

**Scotland: Myth, Legend & Folklore**
Stuart McHardy
ISBN 0 946487 69 3  PB  £7.99

**Luath Storyteller: Highland Myths & Legends**
George W Macpherson
ISBN 1 84282 003 6  PB  £5.00

**Tales of the North Coast**
Alan Temperley
ISBN 0 946487 18 9  PB  £8.99

**Tall Tales from an Island**
Peter Macnab
ISBN 0 946487 07 3  PB  £8.99

**The Supernatural Highlands**
Francis Thompson
ISBN 0 946487 31 6  PB  £8.99

## GENEALOGY

**Scottish Roots: step-by-step guide for ancestor hunters**
Alwyn James
ISBN 1 84282 007 9  PB  £9.99

## WEDDINGS, MUSIC AND DANCE

**The Scottish Wedding Book**
G Wallace Lockhart
ISBN 1 94282 010 9  PB  £12.99

**Fiddles and Folk**
G Wallace Lockhart
ISBN 0 946487 38 3  PB  £7.95

**Highland Balls and Village Halls**
G Wallace Lockhart
ISBN 0 946487 12 X  PB  £6.95

## POETRY

**Bad Ass Raindrop**
Kokumo Rocks
ISBN 1 84282 018 4  PB  £6.99

**Caledonian Cramboclink: the Poetry of**
William Neill
ISBN 0 946487 53 7  PB  £8.99

**Men and Beasts: wild men & tame animals**
Val Gillies & Rebecca Marr
ISBN 0 946487 92 8  PB  £15.00

**Luath Burns Companion**
John Cairney
ISBN 1 84282 000 1  PB  £10.00

**Scots Poems to be read aloud**
intro Stuart McHardy
ISBN 0 946487 81 2  PB  £5.00

**Poems to be read aloud**
various
ISBN 0 946487 00 6  PB  £5.00

## CARTOONS

**Broomie Law**
Cinders McLeod
ISBN 0 946487 99 5  PB  £4.00

## FICTION

**The Road Dance**
John MacKay
ISBN 1 84282 024 9  PB  £9.99

**Milk Treading**
Nick Smith
ISBN 0 946487 75 8  PB  £9.99

**The Strange Case of RL Stevenson**
Richard Woodhead
ISBN 0 946487 86 3  HB  £16.99

**But n Ben A-Go-Go**
Matthew Fitt
ISBN 1 84282 014 1  PB  £6.99

**But n Ben A-Go-Go**
Matthew Fitt
ISBN 0 946487 82 0  HB  £10.99

**Grave Robbers**
Robin Mitchell
ISBN 0 946487 72 3  PB  £7.99

**The Bannockburn Years**
William Scott
ISBN 0 946487 34 0  PB  £7.95

**The Great Melnikov**
Hugh MacLachlan
ISBN 0 946487 42 1  PB  £7.95

## LANGUAGE

**Luath Scots Language Learner [Book]**
L Colin Wilson
ISBN 0 946487 91 X  PB  £9.99

**Luath Scots Language Learner [Double Audio CD Set]**
L Colin Wilson
ISBN 1 84282 026 5  CD  £16.99

## **Luath** Press Limited
*committed to publishing well written books worth reading*

LUATH PRESS takes its name from Robert Burns, whose little collie Luath (*Gael.*, swift or nimble) tripped up Jean Armour at a wedding and gave him the chance to speak to the woman who was to be his wife and the abiding love of his life. Burns called one of *The Twa Dogs* Luath after Cuchullin's hunting dog in *Ossian's Fingal*. Luath Press grew up in the heart of Burns country, and now resides a few steps up the road from Burns' first lodgings in Edinburgh's Royal Mile.

Luath offers you distinctive writing with a hint of unexpected pleasures.

Most UK bookshops either carry our books in stock or can order them for you. To order direct from us, please send a £sterling cheque, postal order, international money order or your credit card details (number, address of cardholder and expiry date) to us at the address below. Please add post and packing as follows: UK – £1.00 per delivery address; overseas surface mail – £2.50 per delivery address; overseas airmail – £3.50 for the first book to each delivery address, plus £1.00 for each additional book by airmail to the same address. If your order is a gift, we will happily enclose your card or message at no extra charge.

**Luath** Press Limited
543/2 Castlehill
The Royal Mile
Edinburgh EH1 2ND
Scotland
Telephone: 0131 225 4326 (24 hours)
Fax: 0131 225 4324
email: gavin.macdougall@luath.co.uk
Website: www.luath.co.uk